CONTENTS

MUSIC WHEN
SOFT VOICES DIE

BY

JOHN KEIR CROSS

British Library Cataloguing-in-Publication Data
A catalogue record for this book is available from the
British Library

JOHN KEIR CROSS

John Keir Cross was born in Scotland in 1911. He worked as an insurance clerk, and may even have been homeless for a portion of his life, working as a travelling ventriloquist to make ends meet before turning to writing. Throughout his life he frequently wrote under the pseudonyms Stephen MacFarlane and Susan Morley. Although most of Cross' fiction was aimed at children, in his day he was quite a sought-after writer of supernatural fiction. His 1944 collection *The Other Passenger* is particularly popular, containing one of his most widely anthologised stories, 'The Glass Eye', in which a ventriloquist is confused with his dummy, as well as 'Esmeralda', 'Hands' and 'Music When Soft Voices Die'. *Mr Bosanko: And Other Stories*, published in the same year, is also relatively well-known. Of the nine novels he penned, Cross' *The Angry Planet* was probably his most successful. Towards the end of his life, Cross was co-writer on the daily radio show *The Archers* for five years, and edited a number of anthologies of horror stories.

MUSIC WHEN SOFT VOICES DIE . . .

SIR ARTHUR CONAN DOYLE

I

I heard of the death of Sir Simon Erskine some five years ago, when I was taking a long holiday in my beloved Scotland. I had known him quite well – a terrible man, moody, powerful, irascible. They said he was only forty-eight when he died. Yet, when I had last seen him, about two years before, at the time of the tragic death of his young wife, he had seemed at least eighty. I remember him then, standing in the porch of that huge, bleak house of his, a brooding and lonely figure, holding tight about him the black cloak he favoured, his already white hair blowing round his temples in the eternal winds of that wild corner of Perthshire. He was the last survivor of the Pitvrackie Erskines – the Black Erskines, as they had been called in the old Covenanting days: stern, merciless, religious men, who believed (if truth be faced) in hellfire and damnation and not much else. It was one of the Black Erskines who, with one mad stroke, had swept the head from the shoulder of a young officer who, in his cups, had questioned some religious truths. And another of the clan, on discovering his wife in adultery, had hanged the woman with his own hands, after immolating her lover most dreadfully before her eyes. A terrible, half-beastly family they were, with a long history of bloodshed and cruelty behind them.

About a month after the death of Sir Simon, the factors announced an auction of his properties and effects at Vrackie Hall. I was sufficiently interested to travel in the creaking old bus from Perth to Pitvrackie that day: not only was I keen to see the curious old house again on its storm-swept promontory among the hills, but there was the chance of picking up a treasure or two. Sir Simon had been a man of many accomplishments. He had been interested in a thousand things – in seventeenth-century Dutch painting, in Romantic English literature of the late eighteenth and early nineteenth centuries, and, above all, in unusual musical instruments. He had, too, done much big game hunting in Africa. It was in Africa, in fact, that he met Bridgid Cannell, whom he later married, and whose strange death affected him so terribly. Indeed, let me be honest and say that it affected him almost to the point of madness. There were wild tales of his behaviour during the last two lonely years

of his life – tales of how he shut himself up for days on end
in the big library of Vrackie Hall, of how the scared servants
heard him sometimes weeping aloud, sometimes laughing,
and sometimes, as it were in a disconsolate frenzy, beating
on a collection of native drums he had brought back from
one of his African expeditions. The wild, primitive rhythms,
going on through the hours and throbbing into the farthest
corners of the dark house, hypnotised him, perhaps, into
forgetting his bitterness and the terrible sense of his loss.
He was a man whose mind was delicately enough poised as
it was, God knows – a man who feared loneliness for what
it might do to him, yet who nursed his passions jealously
and secretly. Neither Bridgid nor his first wife had near-
succeeded in fathoming him – it was as if he needed them,
he needed their company and the comfort of their bodies,
yet was unwilling to let them have access to the innermost
parts of him – a Bluebeard who kept one chamber eternally
secret. His first wife, a young Scotswoman of good family,
had, after five years of him, run off incontinently with a
middle- aged American doctor. The fact that she had no
child by him but had been delivered of a son within a year
of meeting the American, weighed bitterly with Sir Simon.
And when Bridgid died childless, so that he saw the line of
the Black Erskines ending with him, he raged vilely against
the destinies: and so shut himself up in the decaying house,

seeing no one, brooding jealously among those priceless possessions of his, weeping like a spoilt child over his failures, beating insanely on those damnable drums and sending the throbbing restless voices of them across the valley and against the forbidding harsh face of old Ben Vrackie itself . . .

I reached the house that day of the sale in a battered, irritable condition. Gusts of wet, mist-laden wind had worried at me as I mounted the mud-raddled roads to the Hall from Pitvrackie. Dull clouds sagged over the peaks of the hills that surrounded the house, the pine forests that flanked my path were silent and evil seeming, heavily adrip with moisture. I saw no one, save, at one point, an old crosseyed tinker who carried, over his shoulder, a long pole slung with dead rabbits, all matted and patchy from the damp. A fawn-coloured, evil-eyed ferret stared at me out of his pocket. I had a fleeting remembrance of an old childhood fear – that ferrets were capable of springing at human throats and sucking the blood there-from: but the beast, I saw, was chained to the tinker's wrist. I gave the man a greeting but he did not reply – passed on his silent way, his squinting eyes fixed on the roadway before him as he walked.

Vrackie Hall stood back from the road in a large park full of trees and gardens that at one time had been carefully laid out. There was a drive of red gravel. The entrance gates were made of elaborate wrought-iron and there were, above the pillars of them, two eagles, staring at each other with their heads turned sideways. They were made of soft stone that had been eaten away by the weathers, so that they seemed to have a frightful and painful disease. The big house itself, built three-quarters of a century ago on the site of the old Erskine Castle, was a mixture of many styles and periods. There was, first, a large porchway flanked with smooth Grecian pillars, the arch of it embellished by a florid frieze consisting of festoons of fruits and flowers with, occasionally in the midst of them, pot-bellied nymphs in modest attitudes. There were festoons above some of the windows too, and many tiles, glazed in yellow and green, with small fat cupids on them and long formal garlands of flowers. The windows themselves were large, and some of them had inset panes of stained glass at each corner. Those on the front of the house had narrow barred shutters in the French style folded back from them, some a dingy cream colour, others painted in flaky green with white underneath. On the south wall there was an exuberant creeper of a rich glossy brown that merged into fresh green at the top and sides; on the back wall there were espalier fruit trees, pegged symmetrically to the lime-eaten bricks. The roof was tiled with slates of varying shapes, some square, others pointed like diamonds and others curved and scalloped – the layers of these last ones looking like enormous fish scales. And on top of all, overtowering the chimneys, was a domed belfry decorated with still more stone festoons and with, inside it, a small rusted bell that had come from an old monastery of St. Fechan, the ruins of which could be seen among the trees in a corner of the park. That old bell had been rung for three days after the death of Bridgid Erskine – not as a sign of mourning: as a last forlorn hope that its clamour, borne out over the hills would guide her back through the thick mountain mist that was her death-pall to the house where her distracted husband awaited her.

It was a hideous house, this home of the Erskines. I had often speculated, in the old days, on how it was possible for a man of Sir Simon's fastidiousness to live among its rococo carvings. But he seemed singularly attached to it – it was, he once sardonically said, an embodiment, a projection of his own over-elaborate and tortured mind.

When I arrived that day at Vrackie Hall for the auction sale it was to find a small silent company already gathered in the big lobby. The auctioneer had not yet appeared – he was, I understood, a Glasgow man, one Gregory, famed for his dry wit. But it appeared to me, as I looked round the group in the dark hall, that he would have little opportunity that day for the exercise of it. There were about a dozen serious-faced men and two women, and they talked quietly together in twos and threes. I recognised some acquaintances – one of

the women was a dealer in Perth, a Miss Logan: I had been
introduced to her the year before in my mother's house.
Standing alone in a corner was an old man I had seen at
several sales in Scotland before (I was, you must understand,
profoundly interested in such things, with an eye for old
tapestries). This man, I had the fancy, came from Dundee,
where he had a business of some strange sort – we none of
us had ever discovered quite what it was, though we knew it
to be lucrative and had the impression that it had something
to do with drawing or designing. His name was Menasseh,
and he was a small, wizened fellow with a large head covered
with an obvious toupee.

I roamed about the tables for some ten minutes. There
were, I could perceive, even at a cursory glance, some
exquisite things. Among the paintings were two miniatures
by Koninck that I coveted instantly, and a small landscape
by Samuel van Hoogstraaten that I would fain have seen in
my rooms in London as a companion to the de Hooch *Study
of a Hillside Town* I had acquired at Christie's a year before.
There were some beautiful vases from the Delft potteries and
a Mortlake tapestry – a copy, unless I was heavily mistaken,
of one of Le Brun's Gobelin cartoons. In a corner I saw a
most masterly carved limewood cravat, attributed, according
to the notice on it, to Grinling Gibbons. Among the books
was a first edition of Lewis's *The Monk* and a copy, signed

by Maturin himself, of that strangest of works, *Melmoth the Wanderer*. There were some Blake drawings too, and some of the Master's hand-coloured prints for the *Songs of Innocence*. And among all these beautiful things, curiously out of place even in that strange house, was Erskine's collection of African drums. I shuddered as I looked at them, recalling the man's mad, grief-wracked thumping of them during the last two years of his life. They were, in their way, I suppose, beautiful enough. The largest ones were made of parchment stretched on hollow hardwood trunks, with primitive designs carved round them. There were two enchanting but repulsive small drums, however, that had for sounding boards polished human skulls. I could see, from a close examination of the larger one, the low brow and long cranium of the primitive. The parchments of these (as were also the parchments of some of the large drums) were held tight by means of small carved ivory pegs, driven in at an angle. The stretched surfaces of them bore a design in coloured dyes – a serpent coiled in a curious way: three coils at the tail end, an erratic figure eight in the centre of the body, and two coils again at the head, with the long fangs pointing downwards. It was the mounting of these skull-drums that particularly attracted me. A small hole had been bored in the forehead of each and the end of a long bent bar of chased silver inserted therein, so that the drums inclined at a convenient angle for the player. The drumsticks – long, polished bones – rested in hollows in the bases of the silver bars. Yes, beautiful things in their way, they were, as they stood there on the table beneath Erskine's trophy heads of buffalo and lions and his crossed game rifles. It was impossible not to be fascinated by them, though they contrasted so strangely with the more delicate products of the less barbaric civilisation.

I wandered upstairs, since there still seemed little chance of the arrival of Gregory, the auctioneer. One or two of the buyers were looking at their watches and I heard one of them say something about the 'Glasga" express being late as usual, he supposed. I looked into some of the rooms on the first floor, but most of the portable things had been carried downstairs and the bigger pieces were covered with dust-sheets – they were being sold with the house.

I was standing at the long stained glass window at the end of the corridor looking at the mist-cloaked hills, first through the clear panes and then, to give more interest, through the red and the blue ones, when I heard a step behind me and a cheerful deep voice.

'Hullo, Mr. Ferguson. I didn't know you were coming to the auction or I'd have suggested we travelled up from Perth together.'

I looked round and found myself confronting Miss Logan, the dealer I had met the year before at my mother's house. I greeted her civilly and we stood together chatting – talking of my mother first and of what we had both done since our last meeting, and then going on naturally to the things downstairs and Sir Simon.

'You knew him, didn't you?' the big woman asked, and I nodded.

'Oh yes – quite well. A curious man. Impossible to understand.'

'I met him once,' said Miss Logan thoughtfully. 'He made me very uncomfortable – so bleak and cruel, somehow. I was at school with his first wife, you know.'

I expressed myself as interested – as indeed I was.

'Was she – well, as volatile in those days? I mean – you know how she went off with the American doctor – '

'Oh yes, I know about that,' said Miss Logan quickly. 'No – it was really a most curious thing. She wasn't at all like that at school – rather serious and unenterprising, in fact. I could never quite understand it all . . .'

She fell silent, staring out at the hills. Then she added ruminatively:

'A tragic man – tragic. And the last one of that terrible family. What exactly was the story about his second wife? – do you know it? I've heard odd rumours, of course, but I was in France at the time. I never heard the real truth of what happened to her.'

'Nor did anyone,' I said shortly. 'You're looking now at the only one who does know the truth of it all.'

'What do you mean?' asked Miss Logan, turning for a moment from the window, at which she had been standing firmly implanted in the expensive brogues.

'Ben Vrackie. That old mountain is her graveyard – and her only father confessor. There were two of them, you know,' I went on, 'Bridgid and an old friend of Sir Simon's – a well-educated South African Negro called David Strange, a lawyer, I think. Simon met him in Cape Town about the same time that he met Bridgid. He was holidaying here with the Erskine's and one Sunday afternoon he went out for a walk in the hills with Bridgid. Simon would have gone too but he had a headache and went to lie down instead . . .'

I paused for a moment, looking through the red pane at the clammy mist creeping and twisting round the summit of the old mountain. Then I continued:

'They never returned. They stayed out longer than they had intended, and in the evening one of those sudden and terrible mountain mists came down. Simon sent out search parties – he rang the old bell in the belfry for as long as the mist lasted – three whole days – as some sort of signal to them. But they never came. They must have wandered for miles – you know how it is when you are lost in a fog – and then slipped and fallen into a gully, perhaps. Their bodies were never found . . .'

'Horrible,' said Miss Logan with a shudder. 'And that was it, then . . . It must have been appalling for Sir Simon – appalling!'

I nodded.

'It was. He had set such store on this second marriage – the last of the line, you know. Particularly after the tragic disappointment his first wife had been to him . . .'

We were silent. There came a slight commotion from downstairs and, looking over the banister into the hall, I saw that Gregory had arrived. He was divesting himself of his coat – a large, red-faced man, benevolent in appearance: singularly out of place in that over-crowded room with his big, bucolic personality. He was joking with some of the buyers.

Miss Logan and I went downstairs. The buyers were collecting round the dais that had been set up for Gregory. We joined the solemn, whispering group.

II

I stop my narrative here for a moment. It is not easy for me to write – I am no literary man. The sheer manual labour of setting things down is enormous, to say nothing of the wearing effort of coordinating one's facts and arranging them in reasonable coherence for the reader. The pen moves over the paper, the ink flows, the page fills up. Words and more words, yet somehow all the things one had hoped to say remain unsaid. I sit here at my desk in my sequestered room in London, five hundred miles away from Pitvrackie, struggling to set down something about the beastly things that happened in that hideous house. Why? Is it, with those pothooks on paper, to exorcise the ghosts that have been haunting me since ever I learned the truth about Simon Erskine? I don't know. I only know that for five years I have wanted to do this, I have looked forward to doing this. It may never be read – secretly, I hardly want it to be read. If it is, it can harm no one now. They are all dead – old Samuel Menasseh is dead: even Miss Logan, I learned about six months ago in a letter from my mother, died suddenly of heart-failure in her shop.

And there it all is – all those miles away and all those years away. Above my desk now is the van Hoogstraaten landscape I saw and coveted that day of the sale at Vrackie Hall. I bite the end of my pen as I contemplate it. It stands as a symbol for all the horror I have felt through the years – it is impossible for me to look at the peaceful hillside scene without thinking of old Ben Vrackie as I saw him that day through the stained glass with the blood-red mists all about him. And I seem to hear, in my heart, a throbbing echo of the forlorn music thumped out in the empty, soulless rooms of Vrackie Hall by the grief-torn man who was, so tragically against his will, the last of the Black Erskines . . . Well, it is all an old tale now – older with the writing of it, whether that writing is good or ill. How should I know how best to set the story down? How should I know how to arrange in sequence that will give the utmost dramatic value to them? I may emphasise unimportant things, I may hold back on things that should be thrown into relief. I am not a professional. I write for one reason and for one reason only – because I must.

So. I light a cigarette. I return to Vrackie Hall on that day of the auction.

We stood round Gregory, the auctioneer, in a small depressed group. Bidding was good, though the scene was so curiously lifeless in the grey light that came in from the hills through the big windows. Gregory made some valiant efforts to exercise his famous wit, but we were unresponsive – his voice rolled away into the recesses of the hall and the stairway. In the end he gave up. He became mechanical. He lowered his voice, he took to nodding and signalling, the tap of his gavel was almost inaudible. I lost interest after I had bought the van Hoogstraaten and the Mortlake tapestry I had my eye on. I wandered away from the group of bidders and began to glance through the books. I was turning over the leaves of an early copy of *Vathek* when my eye was distracted by the figure of the strange old man, Menasseh.

He was standing a little to my left, before the table displaying Sir Simon's big game trophies. His attitude was one of extreme horror – yet the horror was grotesque: his small wizened body was rigid, so that the musty black cloth of his coat was stretched tight across his shoulder-blades, his pale eyes seemed to protrude, his toupee had slipped a little awry, giving him an irrelevantly rakish aspect. I went on observing him for some time, then moved over beside him.

'Good morning, sir,' I said. 'You seem, like myself, to have lost interest in the proceedings over there.'

He started, then, adjusting his old wire-frame spectacles with, I noticed, a trembling hand, he said:

'Yes . . . I – I'm afraid I have. I . . .'

His voice trailed away. He glanced back at the table and I followed his gaze – to the drums that were among the African trophies. He coughed, then he suddenly took off his glasses altogether and started to polish them with an old silk handkerchief.

'I know you sir,' he said quaveringly, 'I've seen you before
– several times.'

'I'm often in Scotland,' I replied. 'And when I'm in Scotland
I'm often at the sales. My name is Ferguson. I know that
your name is Menasseh – I've seen you frequently too. I take
it you're a dealer? – or are you only an amateur, as I am?'

'Eh?' he stammered (it was as if his mind were not focusing
properly – he was thinking all the time of something else).
'No – not a dealer. Only an amateur, Mr. Ferguson.'

He put on his spectacles again and stared back at the
drums on the table. His gaze was particularly drawn to the
two small drums with the silver mountings. He passed his
hand over his brow – his toupee fell even further askew.

'Horrible – horrible,' he muttered. 'God of Abraham, it's
horrible . . .'

He seemed to go into a trance for a moment or two. Then
he put out his finger and traced, with the trembling point of
it, the singular design of the coiled serpent on the parchment
of the small drums. I watched him, fascinated.

'Hideously attractive things,' I said, by the way of an
opening. 'Typical of Sir Simon to have had them – a man of
curious tastes. You know how he is said to have beaten on
them frantically for hours on end after the disappearance of
his second wife?'

'Yes,' said Menasseh, in a whisper. 'Yes. I know . . .'

'A strange sign of grief.' (I was still searching to bring him out – he was, there was no doubt, affected to the very roots by something.)

'A strange sign of grief indeed,' he muttered, then once more he fell distrait. It was a long time before he added, in an almost inaudible undertone: 'A terrible sign of grief – terrible and horrible . . .'

I looked at him, drawing my brows together. He was white. He kept moistening his thin lips with the point of a colourless tongue. I wanted extremely to ask him what it was that was upsetting him, yet after all I hardly knew him. I found myself, in the long silence that ensued after his last remark, wondering who he was and what he did (I had forgotten, when I asked him if he was a dealer, how, in the old days, we had speculated on his occupation.) Printing, was it – or drawing? Something of that nature, I recalled. Perhaps it was a little publishing business? Yet it was more than likely I would know of it if it was publishing: that was my own line of business – I knew most of the trade in Scotland. Whatever it was it was lucrative – I remembered having heard that he was a wealthy old fellow.

Suddenly we became aware – simultaneously – that two of Gregory's assistants were moving towards us. Apparently the African trophies were next item on the catalogue. I glanced quickly at Menasseh.

'Now's the time,' I said smiling. 'You seem interested in these drums of Erskine's. They're going up, I fancy. Are you buying?'

He gazed at me, his eyes large behind the thick glass of his spectacles.

'Oh no,' he whispered. 'Oh no. God forbid it . . .'

The two men in green baize aprons were lifting some of the larger drums, preparatory to carrying them over to Gregory's dais. Menasseh, I saw by this time, was looking quickly backwards and forwards in an access of nervous apprehension of some sort. He suddenly leaned close up to me.

'Ferguson,' he said, 'I can't keep it, I can't. I must tell someone. I want to see you – I must see you.'

'We could go outside,' I said, a little disturbed, I had to confess, by his urgency. 'I shall not be bidding again. Will you?'

'No. No. Not here,' he muttered. 'Not here – I can't stay here. It has upset me too much – I must go away from here, quickly.'

He fumbled in his waistcoat pocket and thrust a card into my hand.

'If you are in Dundee,' he said, 'if you should be in Dundee – '

'I have to be there at the end of this week, as it happens,'

I answered. 'I have a little business which I am mixing with my holiday. Thursday, I should say – or possibly Friday.'

'Good. Good. Then could you call on me? For God's sake could you call on me?'

I nodded: and he, in his nervousness, set his old head nodding up and down too. I fingered his card, looking at the address on it:

SAMUEL MENASSEH
39, THE PORTWAY
DUNDEE

'My business address,' he said, reading my thoughts. 'But come anytime, anytime this week. I shall be there. I have a little room behind the shop where I live – I only go to my house outside the city at weekends and so on.' Then, reading my thoughts still more deeply, he added: 'My business is strange – very strange. Don't be surprised. It's a little – unpleasant. I don't tell people about it – I won't mention it here . . . But come, sir – oh for God's sake I beg you to come! It will haunt me, this – I'll have no peace!'

He said these last words quickly, in a hoarse, strained whisper. Then he turned and was gone. I was left holding his card, staring after him as he hastened over to the massive door. He had left me with an intolerable curiosity – a sense of dismay over his hurried and half-finished sentences.

I was brought back to my senses by the deep, healthy tones of Miss Logan's voice. She was standing, a sane, coherent figure in her brogues and tweed costume, watching the men as they carried the little skull-drums to Gregory's dais.

'Ferguson,' she called. 'Come quickly. Look at these – they're lovely. I'm having these – by Jove, I'm certainly having these.'

I slipped the old man's card into my pocket and went over to join her. She was by this time holding the smaller drum up to the light and examining the silver base.

'Look here,' she said excitedly. 'What an odd thing. Someone's scratched some verse on the silver – look at it, Shelley of all strange things!'

She read out solemnly:

'Music, when soft voices die,
Vibrates in the memory . . .'

And she laughed.

'Odd thing to find on the mounting of an African drum, I must say. Your old Sir Simon was a devilish queer fish, if ever there was one . . .'

I had to agree. Above all I have to agree to that . . .

III

Almost midnight, incredible how quickly the time has gone. I started writing shortly before seven, and since then have interrupted myself only for long enough to brew some tea at about ten. My pen hand is cramped and painful and my eyes ache terribly from staring at the white paper. Yet I cannot stop – I must go on now.

I look back at what I have written. I feel a sinking in the stomach. How imperfectly I have set things down! A rambling introduction, too much description, a conversation which, on paper, seems disjointed and insane. Yet I have tried faithfully enough to keep a clear head over this nightmare. I have tried to set things in their order, to conjure up some sense of atmosphere. The old house, the death of Bridgid and David Strange in the terrible hill mist, the tragic last months of that haunted, lost man . . . You see, I know it all now, I know every shade of it. And this informs every word I write, every thought I have in this quiet room. My pen moves over the paper slowly and carefully – I stop to think before every word. I know all of it – all of it . . .

My remembrances go, irrelevantly, to Miss Logan. By her very inconsequence in this nightmare she is the most grotesque figure of them all. Tweeds, brogues, untinted lipsalve. The more select journals, the Scottish Nationalist movement, long walks on the moors with one of those sticks

with spikes on the end and handles that fold open to form
a little seat. And her shop with the Chelsea china, the old
spinning wheels, the pictures on wood, the churchwarden
pipes in bundles, the little ornamental shepherd crooks of
green Nailsea glass. And somewhere among all these things,
tucked away in a corner, perhaps, when her first enthusiasm
for them had waned, the little drums. I do not suppose she
even knew of those insane weeping fits of Sir Simon's, when
he sent the sound of those drums across the valley . . .

She had met him once, I remember she said. He had made
her uncomfortable. She had been at school with his first wife.
A quiet girl. She had never been able to understand –

What? How *could* she understand? Miss Logan in her little
shop, dying of heart failure. Yet had her heart ever started?
A man to her was a companion for a walk on the moors.
Of course she had never been able to understand, with her
babbling of Shelley. How could she?

No matter, though. She had her shop with its green Nailsea
glass. And over the door of it, in gilt, old-style lettering, one
word: *Antiques.*

And now, as I near the end of the story, I think of another
shop, a stranger shop. I found it, in the twilight, in a side-
street near the docks in Dundee. It was low-fronted, ill-lit
by a flickering gas standard at the kerb of the pavement. The
window had nothing in it, above the door was no sign to

announce the trade or occupation of its tenant. The name, no more, in faded block capitals:

SAMUEL MENASSEH

I knocked, and heard the echo of my knock go rolling into the dust and darkness inside. I waited, impatient. A sailor stumbled in the dusk farther along the street, singing in the drawn-out, lugubrious tones of a drunken man. I knocked again, and from inside this time there came the sound of shuffling feet and the undoing of a chain.

He seemed smaller now, the old man, as I looked down on him from the pavement. He wore a loose, grey-wool cardigan and, on his head, instead of the toupee, was a skullcap of black velvet – a little biretta of the sort the cantors wear in the synagogues. I greeted him and he nodded. Then he motioned me to follow him and I went inside.

It would be a mockery to say that I was not, in all desperation, impatient and curious. I remembered too acutely the old man's broken conversation in the hall at Vrackie, the whole sense of dismay and nervous horror that had come from him. In the intervening days since that interview I had seen too often, in my mind's eye, that white wizened face, those long trembling fingers of parchment tracing the design of the snake on the other parchment of the drums. I was consumed by impatience. As I followed him through the dim corridor to the sitting-room at the back of the shop, I searched feverishly about me for some sign, some illumination of the mystery of him. But there was nothing. Halfway along the corridor we passed an open door that led into the shop proper. I peered anxiously through it. Dimly glimpsed in the light from the gas standard outside as it flickered through the window, was a counter, exceptionally low. Suspended above it from the ceiling was a long, flexible, snake-like thing – a piece of gas tubing I thought at first, and then had the curious fancy that it was a drill – the cable lead of a pedal drill, such as old-fashioned dentists use. But fantastic to suppose that the man was a dentist. Besides, I had no more than glimpsed the appliance in the gloom . . .

We reached the small sitting-room. I stood for a moment opening and shutting my eyes, accustoming them to the light that came from the gas-bracket above the mantelshelf. The room was poorly furnished – a table, a basket-chair by the fireplace, an old dresser, a wardrobe. In the corner a divan bed. Some books in a hanging shelf, a fretwork pipe-rack. And for pictures –

I, so accustomed to the beautiful in pictures, so used to the shaded tones, the colours in harmony, the designs so subtle, so balanced – all the magic of the Masters: I, with my fastidious passion for tapestries and delicate needlework panels – what could I make of the monstrous things on the walls of that room of Menasseh's? Unframed, stuck to the plaster with rusted drawing pins, glazed with layers of size varnish – those rioting tortured dragons in wild reds and blues, those posies of purple flowers, those bleeding hearts transfixed with arrows, those fleshy nudes in violent pink, with bellies sagged and scarlet-nippled breasts – what could I make of them? And yet, I knew that I knew them – they were, in their style, unmistakable. I searched my memory and then, in a moment, could have laughed aloud. For I had, by a wild coincidence, been thinking just outside, while I had listened to the drunken sailor go stumbling along the street – as it goes, you will understand, when one's mind wanders inconsequently in its own secret places and among old associations – I had been thinking then of a fascination of my childhood: whether that sailor were, as had been the only sailor I had known as a child – tattooed! And I understood the meaning of the drill that hung from the ceiling of Menasseh's shop – I had an image of the dye-charged needle at the end of it stabbing again and again into white, tight flesh.

I turned and looked at the old man.

'Yes,' he nodded. 'Not pleasant, not pleasant. Not a very – *select* job, tattooing. I keep it a secret. I have money, you see – it makes money for me. I can gratify my passions for the beautiful things in the sale-rooms. You should see my house outside the town – beautiful, beautiful. Different from this,' he added, sweeping his arm vaguely round the room. 'Oh different, much different . . . But it makes money, this. You haven't an idea – the people who want it – big men: lawyers – I did a lawyer from Glasgow last week – he came up specially. Women too. I'm busy – all the time. There's a sort of fascination in it for some people – all sorts of strange and unexpected people . . .'

He went on, rubbing his hands together. It was incredible and fantastic – too much. But at the back of my mind was beginning to throb the idea that has haunted me through these years. On the table in that little room, smaller than those other charts on the walls, but like them painted in brilliant water colours and covered with size, was a design I had seen before. A serpent coiled in a curious way: three coils at the tail end, an erratic figure eight in the centre of the body, and two coils again at the head, with the long fangs pointing downwards . . .

Half-past one. Almost finished. A century, since I started to write. How did it go? –

'I heard of the death of Sir Simon Erskine some five years ago . . . I had known him quite well – a terrible man, moody, powerful, irascible . . .'

I had known him quite well . . . How did I dare to write

that? How could I – or anyone – know him? No one in the world – no one but those half-beast forebears of his. And they, thank God, have gone out of the world – as he has. The line of the Black Erskines is ended, and for ever.

I look at the quiet picture above me. Samuel van Hoogstraaten – a still man, unperturbed. His world a hillside scene in Holland: small square houses, lines on canvas. To my right, on the wall there, is the Mortlake tapestry. And what association have these things with the things Menasseh told me in that room of his behind the shop? . . .

David Strange, the young Negro lawyer – the descendant, he claimed, of Kings Cetewayo and Dingaan; for he had, as he showed Menasseh, the royal serpent of the Zulus needled into the dark skin of his breast. And the woman with him in the shop that day, with Menasseh copying the design on to *her* breast, while she flinched at every needle-prick, holding tight with her white hand to the dark hand of the Negro . . . . The sign of blood-kinship among the Zulus, that serpent. Menasseh had been intrigued by the design of it and had made, on paper, one copy: but no other copy, at any time, on any human skin but hers . . .

My hand aches terribly. I sit back. I look at my fingers as I stretch them out to ease them . . .

I think – oh God knows what I think! Of the two skulls that were the sounding boards of those hellish drums. Of

Miss Logan tramping over the moors. Of those other two – of blood-kinship – setting off that Sunday afternoon for a walk on Ben Vrackie. Of Sir Simon saying he had a headache and so being unable to accompany them. Of the neat round holes in the skulls in which were inserted the ends of the silver mounts. Of the rifles on the walls of Vrackie Hall. Of the bodies that were never found. Of the shape of the larger skull, the low brow and long cranium of the primitive – the Negro. Of the merciful hill mist that came down on the grim old mountain – red and terrible seen through the glass of that hideous house . . .

Yes, what do I think . . .

Of the two last years of the last of the Erskines, his fits of weeping, his fits of laughing, his fits of –

No. The image fades. The ghost goes out of me. I think of nothing. Except, coming over the years, the echo, terrible in this quiet room, of Miss Logan's cheerful voice:

'Someone's scratched some verse on the silver – Shelley, of all strange things . . .'

Yes. Shelley, of all strange things.

www.ingramcontent.com/pod-product-compliance
Lightning Source LLC
Chambersburg PA
CBHW050324200626
46810CB00022B/1992